The Tiara Club

at Pearl Palace

For Princess Hannah and her magic
grandmother, Queen Val
VF
With special thanks to JD

www.tiaraclub.co.uk

ORCHARD BOOKS
338 Euston Road, London NW1 3BH
Orchard Books Australia
Level 17/207 Kent St, Sydney, NSW 2000
A Paperback Original
First published in 2007 by Orchard Books
Text © Vivian French 2007
Cover illustration © Sarah Gibb 2007
Inside illustrations © Orchard Books 2007

A CIP catalogue record for this book is available
from the British Library.

ISBN 978 1 84616 498 9

3 5 7 9 10 8 6 4 2

Printed in Great Britain
The paper and board used in this paperback are natural recyclable
products made from wood grown in sustainable forests. The
manufacturing processes conform to the environmental
regulations of the country of origin.

Orchard Books is a division of Hachette Children's Books,
an Hachette Livre UK company.
www.orchardbooks.co.uk

The Tiara Club

at Pearl Palace

Princess Hannah

and the Little Black Kitten

By Vivian French

ORCHARD BOOKS

The Royal Palace Academy
for the Preparation of Perfect Princesses

(Known to our students as "*The Princess Academy*")

OUR SCHOOL MOTTO:
A Perfect Princess always thinks of others
before herself, and is kind, caring and truthful.

Pearl Palace offers a complete education for Tiara Club princesses with emphasis on the arts and outdoor activities. The curriculum includes:

A special Princess Sports Day

A trip to the Magical Mountains

Preparation for the Silver Swan Award (stories and poems)

A visit to the King Rudolfo's Exhibition of Musical Instruments

Our headteacher, King Everest, is present at all times, and students are well looked after by the head fairy godmother, Fairy G, and her assistant, Fairy Angora.

Our resident staff and visiting experts include:

QUEEN MOLLY (Sports and games)

LADY MALVEENA (Secretary to King Everest)

LORD HENRY (Natural History)

QUEEN MOTHER MATILDA (Etiquette, Posture and Flower Arranging)

We award tiara points to encourage our Tiara Club princesses towards the next level. All princesses who win enough points at Pearl Palace will be presented with their Pearl Sashes and attend a celebration ball.

Pearl Sash Tiara Club princesses are invited to go on to Emerald Castle, our very special residence for Perfect Princesses, where they may continue their education at a higher level.

PLEASE NOTE:
Pets are not allowed at Pearl Palace.
Princesses are expected to arrive at
the Academy with a *minimum* of:

TWENTY BALLGOWNS
(with all necessary hoops,
petticoats, etc)

TWELVE DAY DRESSES

SEVEN GOWNS
suitable for garden parties,
and other special
day occasions

TWELVE TIARAS

DANCING SHOES
five pairs

VELVET SLIPPERS
three pairs

RIDING BOOTS
two pairs

Cloaks, muffs, stoles, gloves
and other essential
accessories as required

Hello! I'm Princess Hannah, and I'm SO pleased you're here at Pearl Palace with me. Isabella, Lucy, Grace, Ellie and Sarah are thrilled as well – have you met them yet? They're my friends in Lily Room, and we do everything together. I'm really looking forward to our new term – although I do hope the twins aren't TOO dreadful. You just never know what they'll think of next...

Chapter One

Isn't it just so exciting when you wake up somewhere new? My first ever morning at Pearl Palace was like that. I opened my eyes, and there I was in Lily Room, with all my very best friends.

I sat up in bed and looked round. Lucy had her head under her pillow like she always does,

and Sarah was asleep on her back with her mouth open. Grace and Isabella were asleep as well, but Ellie was sitting on the edge of her bed. She smiled when she saw I was awake.

"Isn't this room LOVELY?" she said. "We've never had lily wallpaper before."

"We did have lily-patterned curtains when we were in Silver Towers," I reminded her.

"This is MUCH nicer," Ellie said firmly, and I couldn't help agreeing with her.

Grace yawned, and threw back her covers. "Isn't it brilliant to be together again? I missed you all so much during the holidays."

"Me too," I said, and Ellie nodded.

"I didn't miss Diamonde and Gruella, though," Grace went on.

"Do you think they'll be as horrid as ever?"

"'A Perfect Princess ALWAYS thinks the best of others,'" Ellie quoted. She pulled at Lucy's pillow, and tweaked Sarah's and Isabella's covers. "Wake up, everyone! It's a brand new term!"

"Oof!" Lucy rubbed her eyes. "Hello, Ellie! Hello, every—"

BANG!

Lucy was interrupted by a loud knock on the door, and Fairy G, the Royal Academy fairy godmother, burst in.

"LILY ROOM!" she bellowed. "What ARE you doing? The bell

rang AGES ago and you're all late for breakfast!"

We stared at her in complete astonishment.

"We didn't hear it, Fairy G,"
I said. "Honestly!"

Fairy G shook her head. "Too
much talking last night, I expect!"

We looked at each other guiltily.

We HAD talked quite late...we'd been so excited to meet up again after the holidays.

"You'd better be as quick as you can," Fairy G told us. "Your new headteacher is NOT best pleased. King Everest is a firm believer in the saying, 'A Perfect Princess is ALWAYS on time for every appointment, no matter what it might be.' Hurry downstairs and make sure you say how sorry you are. We don't want you beginning the new term with minus tiara points!" And Fairy G stamped out of the door.

We absolutely flew to the bathroom before tumbling into our clothes. After grabbing our tiaras we rushed out of Lily Room, and along the corridor and down the stairs. We were halfway

down when Sarah stopped so suddenly we all piled into each other in the MOST unprincessy way.

"Sarah!" I gasped. "What ARE you doing?"

"SH!" she said. "Listen!"

"We haven't time to listen," I said crossly, but Lucy grabbed my arm. "I can hear it too!"

"And me!" Ellie froze. "It's a cat – and it sounds SO unhappy."

"LOOK!" Isabella pointed back up the staircase. "There – on the top of the cupboard by the window! It's the SWEETEST little black kitten!"

"I think it's stuck!" Grace's eyes opened very wide. "Oh, the poor little thing!"

"We have to help it," I said. "Lily Room to the rescue!"

Chapter Two

As we dashed back up the stairs towards the cupboard we could see the kitten's big anxious eyes staring down at us.

"We mustn't frighten it," Lucy whispered.

"However did it get there?" Ellie asked. "It's really high up."

"Maybe it climbed up the

curtains and jumped across,"
Sarah suggested.

Grace had reached the cupboard
and was making little soothing
noises at the kitten. It looked
back at her with its head on one
side as if it knew we were trying to

help. Lucy pulled up a chair, and I climbed on and reached up.

The kitten was SO sweet! It had the softest fluffy black fur, and huge blue eyes, and it snuggled into my arms as I lifted it down. Isabella tickled it behind its ears and it began to purr loudly.

"Oooh!" Grace breathed. "Isn't it GORGEOUS? Do you think we could keep it?"

"We could call it Lily!" I said.

"Brilliant!" Ellie patted me on the back, and at exactly that moment a bell rang loudly just above our heads. The kitten squeaked, jumped out of my arms

21

and zoomed away down the corridor at a million miles per hour. I was about to rush after it when Lucy caught me by the hand.

"Hannah!" she said, and her face was very pale. "I think that was the after breakfast bell! WE'VE MISSED BREAKFAST ALTOGETHER!"

"Lily Room!" Diamonde's voice called from the bottom of the stairs. "Are you there? King Everest wants to see all of you in his study now, this minute!"

There was a snigger, and Gruella said, "He's FURIOUS!"

"That's right." Diamonde sounded really pleased. "He even said something about sending you home in disgrace, didn't he, Gruella?"

I felt a horrid cold chill in the pit of my stomach.

"So don't think YOU'LL be going to the Pearl Palace Party tonight!" Diamonde added as she and Gruella flounced off.

"Do you think Diamonde's right?" Lucy asked as we trailed

gloomily down the stairs.

"It would be TERRIBLE if she is," Grace sighed. "I do so love the beginning of term parties."

"Don't worry," Ellie told her. "I'm sure it'll be OK when we tell him we were rescuing a poor little lost kitten."

"That's right!" Sarah cheered up at once. "What's that bit in the Perfect Princess handbook? 'Perfect Princesses always care for anyone in trouble and distress.' That kitten was certainly in trouble."

Sarah and Ellie are SO wonderful. They always manage to look on the bright side. I was feeling much better as we arrived outside King Everest's study door, and Isabella gave me a nudge.

"Go on, Hannah," she said, "you're brave. You knock!"

So I did. Rat-a-tat-tat! And a stern voice called, "Come in!"

Chapter Three

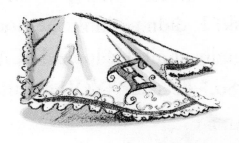

Although we'd arrived at Pearl Palace the day before, we hadn't met King Everest properly. He'd hurried past us while we were in the main hallway sorting out our trunks, but he hadn't stopped to speak to us. Alice from Rose Room had told us who he was, and I'd thought he looked rather nice and friendly – but when we walked into his study and saw him sitting behind his desk I didn't think he looked friendly at all. He looked SCARY!

"So," he said, "YOU are the six

princesses who think you can sleep as late as you like! I hope you have an explanation for your extremely rude behaviour!" And he glared at us.

I swallowed hard, and curtsied.

"If you please, Your Majesty, we DID oversleep, and we're very sorry. When Fairy G called us we hurried as much as we could, but we found a little black kitten stuck on top of the cupboard on the landing and we stopped to rescue it."

"It was SO unhappy," Sarah added.

We all nodded, and looked hopefully at King Everest. Surely he would be pleased with us now – but he wasn't. He positively glowered.

"I have NEVER heard such a foolish excuse!" he roared.

"I'm going to give you twelve minus tiara points each. Two for oversleeping, and ten for telling lies to get yourself out of trouble. And as you chose to miss breakfast, it seems only fair that you also miss the Pearl Palace Party." King Everest stopped, and blew his nose again.

"Consider yourselves VERY lucky that I haven't sent you home. Now, go to the detention room, which is next to the dining hall. Report to Lady Malveena, and tell her I want you to remain there until I have decided you are ready to return to your lessons.

Ah...ah...ah...ATCHOOO!" King Everest sneezed another massive sneeze, and waved us out of his study.

Outside, I found my legs felt really wobbly.

"Oh my goodness!" Lucy gasped. "Wasn't that absolutely DREADFUL?"

The rest of us nodded. We were too depressed to say anything more as we dragged ourselves past the dining hall, and into the detention room.

Lady Malveena was tall and extremely thin, with spectacles balanced on the very end of her long spiky nose. "Good morning, princesses!" she said in the coldest voice. "Please introduce yourselves."

As we told her who we were she wrote our names in a large book. When she had finished she gave a little sniff, and peered at us over her spectacles.

"So YOU are the princesses from Lily Room! I have to say that I'm shocked to see you here. You had an excellent report from Ruby Mansions."

"Please believe us," I said earnestly. "We truly didn't mean to do anything wrong today—"

"That's right!" Grace did her best to smile at Lady Malveena. "We were only trying to help a kitten."

I thought we'd better tell her the whole truth, so I added, "Actually, we DID oversleep – but it was the kitten that held us up."

Lady Malveena folded her arms,

and I could see she didn't believe us. I suddenly felt completely miserable – and I wished and WISHED we could tell Fairy G what had happened. She's known us for ages, and I was sure she would explain to Lady Malveena that none of us would EVER tell lies to get ourselves out of trouble.

To my amazement I'd hardly finished wishing when the detention room door burst open, and Fairy G strode in – but she didn't look as if she'd come to save us. She was HUGE, and she only grows like that when she's angry. VERY angry! She

swept through the door, and bellowed, "Lily Room! King Everest has just told me what you've done! I'm SO disappointed in you!"

Chapter Four

My eyes must have looked as if they were about to pop out of my head. I'd NEVER seen Fairy G so angry. But then something seriously weird happened – I got angry too!

My last report had said that I might not be an absolutely Perfect Princess, but I did always try my best, and I was honest and truthful. If that was what Fairy G thought, why hadn't she waited to hear our side of the story?

I took a deep breath, and stepped forward. "You know what, Fairy G," I said, "that's not fair. We'd NEVER let you down if we could possibly help it. We DID find a kitten, and I'm sorry nobody believes us, but it's the absolute truth. And I'm going to go and find it, just to prove we don't tell lies!" And I actually pushed my way past Fairy G and stomped out of the detention room, my heart hammering in my chest.

I almost expected Fairy G to wave her wand and turn me into a frog or something (not that she's EVER done anything so awful) because I knew I'd been shockingly rude – but I went on walking. Isabella, Grace, Lucy, Ellie, Sarah and I NEVER tell lies – and I was going to prove it. I marched up the stairs to the top landing, and called, "Puss! Puss! Where are you? Puss!"

There was no sign of the kitten in Lily Room. I looked under all the beds, and in the wardrobes. I even looked in our bedside cupboards, but there was no kitten there.

"Puss!" I called again, "PLEASE come out!"

But no kitten appeared.

"Maybe it's hiding in one of the other dormitories," I told myself, and I opened the door next to Lily Room. The wallpaper was covered in roses, so I knew it must be Rose Room – but the kitten wasn't there either. The next door was half-open, and the moment I looked in I realised it was Diamonde and Gruella's room. Even though I was so anxious about the kitten I couldn't help thinking how odd it was that their parents insisted the twins had a room of their own. It was full of mirrors, and a huge portrait of the two of them hung on the wall, and there was another picture of a snooty looking queen. I decided that must be their mother.

I was about to shut the door when I heard a tiny MEEOW! and a ball of black fluff came tottering out from under one of the beds. It meowed again as it came towards me, and it sounded so lonely.

"Lily!" I whispered, and I picked her up and snuggled her under my chin.

"WHAT are you doing in OUR room?" Diamonde and Gruella were standing in the doorway staring at me. I turned, and my foot knocked against something on the floor. I glanced down, and there was a little china bowl half full of kitty crunchies. Beside it was a saucer of milk.

"What...?" I didn't know what to say. "Is...is this YOUR kitten?"

"It belongs to Gruella! SHE brought it here!" Diamonde snapped.

"I SO did not!" Gruella retorted. "It was YOUR idea!"

"Do you know what?" I interrupted. "I don't care which of you brought it here. What I DO care about is Lily Room. You've got us into a whole LOAD of trouble!"

Diamonde made a face. "So what?" She picked up the china bowl and pushed it into my hand. "There! You can keep Tiddles to make up. I'm bored with her. She keeps running off."

"But I'm not! I LOVE little Tiddles!" Gruella wailed.

"Then YOU stop her running away," Diamonde sneered, and she swung round – and found herself face to face with King Everest and Fairy G.

Chapter Five

"ATCHOOO!" As soon as King Everest set eyes on the kitten he began to sneeze. He sneezed and he SNEEZED, and I knew I had to take the kitten away. I ran to the top of the stairs, and saw Ellie hurrying towards me.

"Are you all right?" she asked anxiously. "Lady Malveena said

King Everest was going to send you home!"

"I'm fine!" I said. "Here – take Lily and look after her while I explain what's going on."

I handed the purring kitten over, and rushed back to where King Everest was mopping his nose and wiping his eyes.

"If you please, Your Majesty," I said, "that was the kitten we found this morning."

Our headteacher shook his head. "But how did it get here? Who does it belong to?"

"It's Princess Hannah's kitten, Your Majesty." Diamonde gave me a sly look. "Isn't it, Gruella? Wasn't Hannah showing us his little bowl just a minute ago, and boasting about how she'd hidden him in Lily Room? We were worried she'd

55

make us late for lessons, weren't we Gruella? So now we'd better hurry—" and she grabbed Gruella and headed for the door.

"Just a moment – just a MOMENT!" Fairy G boomed. "Diamonde and Gruella – stay where you are!"

"ATCHOOO!" King Everest began sneezing again, and Fairy G tut-tutted at me, but in quite a friendly way.

"Hannah dear, would you mind standing a little further off? I think the kitten's left fur on your dress, and it's making His Majesty sneeze."

"Oh – I'm so sorry," I said as I backed further down the corridor. A sudden thought popped into my head, and before I could stop myself I said, "So THAT'S why you sneezed when we came to see you this morning, Your Majesty! We'd just been stroking the kitten!"

King Everest tried to answer, but he couldn't stop sneezing.

"It seems to me, Hannah, that I owe you an apology." Fairy G looked at me thoughtfully. "You were quite right to accuse me of not being fair. There really was a kitten here all the time."

"But is it – ATCHOO! – YOUR kitten?" King Everest managed to speak at last. "Did YOU bring it here to Pearl Palace?"

"No, Your Majesty," I said firmly. "I promise I didn't."

"Then who did?" the king asked. "It's much too small a beast to come on its own."

Of course I couldn't answer. I couldn't tell tales, even though Diamonde had tried to blame me. And then I had an idea.

"Maybe, Your Majesty," I suggested as politely as I could, "YOU could discover where the kitten came from?"

"ME?" King Everest looked astonished, but Fairy G began to chuckle – a lovely cheerful noise that made me think everything might turn out all right after all.

"Hannah wants you to pop your head round every dormitory door," she explained. "You'll sneeze as soon as you reach the room where the kitten's been hiding!"

At first I thought King Everest would be angry again, but he wasn't. He was laughing as he strode towards Lily Room.

"Let's clear your good name, young lady," he said as he passed me, and he threw open the door and went in.

Not a sneeze. Not even a very little one.

And he didn't sneeze in Rose Room. Or Poppy Room. Or Tulip or Daffodil. But when he walked into Diamonde and Gruella's room...

"ATCHOOO! ATCHOOOO!
ATCHOOOO! ATCHOOOO!"
He sneezed so long and so hard
Fairy G had to wave her wand.

Twinkling stars whizzed round
King Everest's head, and
he stopped with a final
"AtchWUMPH!"

At first Diamonde did her best to look innocent. "The kitten must have just crawled in here by mistake," she said brightly.

"Perhaps it did," Fairy G agreed. I caught her eye, and she winked at me. "I think we should take it outside, a long way away from here, and let it go."

There was a loud gasp from Gruella. "PLEASE don't! Poor little Tiddles – she wouldn't know what to do." She hung her head. "I'm SO sorry, Fairy G. We couldn't bear to leave her at home, and we thought it would be fun to bring her here to Pearl Palace."

"But pets are strictly forbidden," King Everest said sternly. "Especially – ATCHOO! – cats!" He folded his arms. "I think you and your sister had better take your kitten home this very afternoon, and come back tomorrow. We'll forget this unfortunate incident, and you can make a fresh start."

"But we'll miss the party!" Diamonde sounded outraged, but when she saw King Everest's face she stopped. "Yes, Your Majesty," she whispered. Very quietly she reached under her bed, and pulled out a cat's travelling basket.

"Please," I said, "please – can we say goodbye to Lily? I mean Tiddles?"

Fairy G beamed. "Just as long as you give your hands a good wash afterwards."

"THANK YOU!" I said.

As I turned to hurry away, Fairy G said, "Hannah – you'd better tell the rest of Lily Room that you've still got two minus tiara points for being late, but you've all got ten plus points for being kind and caring. And after you've said goodbye to the kitten you can run down to the ballroom – we're going to have a Pearl Palace Party preparation lesson. I'm going to teach you the Pearl Palace Polka!"

Chapter Six

And that's what we did. And after
we'd learnt how to dance the
polka, we learnt the Pearl Palace
Pirouette – and it was SUCH fun!
We danced until the bell rang for
lunch. We were about to line up
when King Everest came in, and
asked us to be silent for a minute as
he had something important to say.

"Princesses!" he announced, "as I told MOST of you at breakfast—" and his eyes twinkled as he looked across at me and my friends, "I am delighted to welcome you to Pearl Palace. I am, however, especially delighted to discover that I have a princess

here who isn't afraid to speak out in the cause of truth...even if her timekeeping does need a little improvement. Princess Hannah, I hope you and your friends from Lily Room will start the dancing at the party tonight with the Pearl Palace Polka!"

What do you think we said? YES
PLEASE, of course! And we had a
really REALLY brilliant time,

except – do you know what?
I actually missed Diamonde and
Gruella!

But as we were settling down to sleep that night, Grace pointed out it was silly to miss them too much. "After all, they'll be back tomorrow."

"We'd better not talk any more," Sarah said sleepily. "We don't want to miss breakfast again..."

"It'll be OK," Lucy told her. "I've set FOUR alarm clocks!" and we all laughed.

And as I was slipping into sleep I thought, "Pearl Palace is going to be SUCH fun...and do you know what makes it extra special?

"YOU'RE here too!"

What happens next?
Find out in

Princess Isabella
and the Snow-White Unicorn

Dear princess – I'm so very pleased you're here at Pearl Palace with me and all my friends from Lily Room! I'm Princess Isabella; I expect you already know Hannah, Lucy, Grace, Ellie and Sarah. And have you met the twins, Diamonde and Gruella? If you have you'll know what they're like – just awful! Especially when we go out on school trips...

Look out for

Princess Parade

with Princess Hannah and Princess Lucy
ISBN 978 1 84616 504 7

And look out for the Daffodil Room princesses in
the Tiara Club at Emerald Castle:

Princess Amelia and the Silver Seal
Princess Leah and the Golden Seahorse
Princess Ruby and the Enchanted Whale
Princess Millie and the Magical Mermaid
Princess Rachel and the Dancing Dolphin
Princess Zoe and the Wishing Shell

Have you read all the Tiara Club books?

Win a Tiara Club
Perfect Princess Prize!

Look for the secret word in mirror writing that is hidden in a tiara in each of the Tiara Club books. Each book has one word. Put together the six words from books **19** to **24** to make a special Perfect Princess sentence, then send it to us together with 20 words or more on why you like the Tiara Club books. Each month, we will put the correct entries in a draw and one lucky reader will receive a magical Perfect Princess prize!

Send your Perfect Princess sentence,
at least 20 words on why you like the Tiara Club,
your name and your address on a postcard to:
THE TIARA CLUB COMPETITION,
Orchard Books, 338 Euston Road,
London, NW1 3BH

Australian readers should write to:
Hachette Children's Books,
Level 17/207 Kent Street, Sydney, NSW 2000.

Only one entry per child.
Final draw: 30 September 2008

By Vivian French
Illustrated by Sarah Gibb

The Tiara Club

The Tiara Club at Silver Towers

The Tiara Club at Ruby Mansions

The Tiara Club at Pearl Palace

PRINCESS HANNAH
AND THE LITTLE BLACK KITTEN   ISBN   978 1 84616 498 9

PRINCESS ISABELLA
AND THE SNOW-WHITE UNICORN   ISBN   978 1 84616 499 6

PRINCESS LUCY
AND THE PRECIOUS PUPPY   ISBN   978 1 84616 500 9

PRINCESS GRACE
AND THE GOLDEN NIGHTINGALE   ISBN   978 1 84616 501 6

PRINCESS ELLIE
AND THE ENCHANTED FAWN   ISBN   978 1 84616 502 3

PRINCESS SARAH
AND THE SILVER SWAN   ISBN   978 1 84616 503 0

BUTTERFLY BALL   ISBN   978 1 84616 470 5

CHRISTMAS WONDERLAND   ISBN   978 1 84616 296 1

PRINCESS PARADE   ISBN   978 1 84616 504 7

All priced at £3.99.
Butterfly Ball, *Christmas Wonderland* and *Princess Parade* are priced at £5.99.
The Tiara Club books are available from all good bookshops, or can be ordered
direct from the publisher: Orchard Books, PO BOX 29, Douglas IM99 1BQ.
Credit card orders please telephone 01624 836000
or fax 01624 837033 or visit our website: www.orchardbooks.co.uk
or e-mail: bookshop@enterprise.net for details.

To order please quote title, author and ISBN and your full name and address.
Cheques and postal orders should be made payable to 'Bookpost plc.'
Postage and packing is FREE within the UK
(overseas customers should add £2.00 per book).

Prices and availability are subject to change.

Check out

website at:

www.tiaraclub.co.uk

You'll find Perfect Princess games and fun
things to do, as well as news on the Tiara
Club and all your favourite princesses!